PETER PAN

PETER PAN

Illustrated by
GREG HILDEBRANDT

Adapted from the novel by
J.M. Barrie

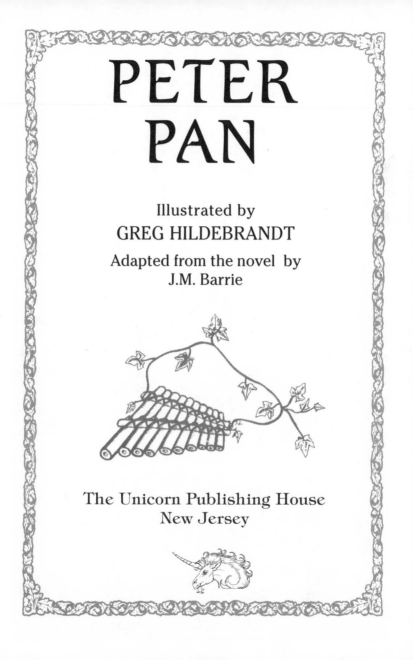

The Unicorn Publishing House
New Jersey

PETER PAN

The Darling family loved to dance. And all of the Darlings would join in. Even Nana, the Darling's dog, loved to twirl about with the children, barking and bounding with joy as they skipped and jumped around her. In fact, the Darlings would dance in the nursery almost every night before the children went to bed. There never was a simpler, happier family in all the world—that is, until Peter Pan came.

You see, *all* children, except one, grow up. And that child is Peter Pan. He lives in a place both far-away and yet very near. He lives in a place called the Neverland. He lives in children's minds. All children know the Neverland, though it is never the same for any two. If you close your eyes very tight, and think of your favorite place—your secret place—there you will find Neverland. It is full of magic and make-believe, just for you, and any adventure you might have a mind to choose. So it was with the Darling children. On the magic shores of Neverland the children often played. And often they played with Peter Pan. Especially Wendy, the oldest.

Mrs. Darling first heard of Peter when she was cleaning up the children's minds. You see, every night, all good mothers rummage through their children's minds after the children have gone to sleep. They put things straight for the next morning. That's why, when you wake up, your prettier thoughts are nicely aired and spread out, waiting for you to put them on for the new day.

In her travels through the children's minds Mrs. Darling found the most confusing name: Peter. She knew of no Peter, yet he was here and there in John and little Michael's minds. Wendy's mind was filled with him. But *who* was Peter?

When Wendy's mother asked her, Wendy simply said, "He is Peter Pan, *you know,* mother." At first Mrs. Darling did not know. But after thinking back to her childhood, she remembered a Peter Pan who was said to live with the fairies.

The next night, Mrs. Darling fell asleep in the nursery while she was sewing. As she dreamed, the window of the nursery blew open. In dropped a boy to the floor. With him was a strange little light that darted about the room like a living thing. It must have been this light that wakened Mrs. Darling. She knew at once that the boy was none other than Peter Pan.

He was a lovely boy, dressed in shining leaves and the sap that seeps out of trees.

When he saw that she was a grown-up, he snarled his pearl-like teeth at her. Mrs. Darling screamed. The door opened and Nana ran in. She growled and sprang at the boy, who leaped lightly through the window and vanished like a shooting

star. But Peter didn't make a clean escape altogether, for you see, Nana caught his shadow. Mrs. Darling didn't know what to do, so she rolled Peter's shadow up and placed it in a drawer till she could talk to her husband.

The next night the Darlings were invited to dinner next door. As soon as the Darlings left, a small star in the sky cried out: "Now, Peter!" In a flash, Peter came through the nursery window and began searching for his shadow.

But when he found it, he couldn't get it to
stick on. Poor Peter began to cry. His crying woke
Wendy. She looked with wonder at the strange boy
and then saw a tiny light darting about, which
suddenly stopped, revealing a fairy.

"I'm Peter Pan, and my fairy is called Tinker Bell." "My name is Wendy, and this is John and Michael." Wendy sewed Peter's shadow to his feet, and he was so happy that he sprinkled everyone with fairy dust and they began to fly!

"Would you like to fly to Neverland with me?" Peter asked. "We would! We would!" the three cried with joy. "Hurry, Peter!" Tinker Bell called to him. The Darlings were coming home, but it *was* too late. The birds had flown.

"Second to the right, and straight on till morning." That, Peter had said, was the way to Neverland. But as they reached the magic shores the pirates shot a cannonball at them, the wind of which scattered the children far, far apart.

Wendy had been holding Tinker Bell in John's hat when the ball flew by, so she found herself alone with the fairy. Tinker Bell was jealous of Wendy. Peter liked her. She *knew* it. So Tink popped out of the hat and began making trouble.

Meanwhile, the pirates were out looking for Peter and the lost boys. The lost boys are Peter's friends. And Peter is their leader. The pirates had a leader, too. The very evil Captain Hook. He wanted to catch Peter very badly. But there was

something that wanted to catch Hook. *Tick-tick-tick!* That was the sound Hook feared most. The sound of the crocodile that bit his hand off, and liked the taste so much, it had followed him ever since. The *tick* was really a clock the crocodile had

eaten, but it warned Hook when it was near. While
the pirates looked for Peter, Tink *did* a terrible
thing. She found the lost boys and told them
Wendy was a bird and that Peter had said to shoot
her. And they did!

Down came Wendy to the ground with an arrow in her chest. The lost boys knew they had been tricked by Tink. One of the boys cried: "This is no bird! I think it must be a lady." And another said: "And we have killed her! Peter was bringing her to us to be our mother. And now we have killed her!"

But they hadn't killed her. When Peter arrived, he saw at once that the arrow had been stopped by a present he had given Wendy. A magic acorn. She had worn it on a chain around her neck. It *had* saved her life.

Then the lost boys told Peter of Tink's crime.

"Tinker Bell," he shouted, "I am your friend no more." And he wouldn't speak to her for a whole week.

Wendy was weak from her fall and needed to be cared for at once. Peter decided they should build a house for her. John and Michael arrived and were put to work also on the little hut. They didn't like having to be *so* good to their big sister, but Peter insisted.

You see, the lost boys are exactly that. Lost. For one reason or another, they became separated from their mothers, and with no one to care for them, they arrive in Neverland where they can care for each other. But Peter now had the idea that Wendy *could be* their mother. She could tell them stories, make them all take their medicine, and tuck them in bed at night.

When Wendy awoke, she was very surprised to see the little hut they had built for her. And when they asked her to be their mother, she said:

"Should I? It's very thrilling, but I'm *only* a little girl." But Peter said they just needed the nice motherly type. "In that case, I will do my best. Come inside at once, you naughty children." And the boys gleefully did as they were told.

And that was the first of many happy evenings. At night, Wendy would tuck the boys in a great bed in their *secret* cave. Wendy would sleep in the hut as Peter kept watch outside. During the night only tiny fairies crossed his path as they made their

way homeward.

Wendy proved to be a good mother. In their underground hideout she told them stories, made them keep their cave clean, and gave them their medicine (which was really sugar-water).

Adventures, of course, happened daily. But there is one, above all, I must tell. The children often spent their day at the Mermaid's Lagoon. The mermaids were never seen, except after a rain, when they played with bubbles of rainwater. On

this day, they could not be found. As evening fell,
the children were resting on Marooner's Rock,
when Peter suddenly jumped to his feet and cried:
"Pirates!" A boat drew near. Peter saw at once the
pirates had a prisoner.

The pirates had captured Tiger Lily, the proud princess of the Indian tribe. Two pirates brought her ashore just as the children slipped into the water to hide. Peter knew what the pirates would do. With Tiger Lily bound tight with rope, they would leave her on the rock for the tide to come in and drown her. But Peter Pan would never let that happen. Calling out to the pirates in the darkness, he sounded just like Captain Hook, shouting: "Ahoy there, ahoy there you lubbers!" It was a wonderful job.

"The captain!" said one of the pirates. "He must be swimming here. Ahoy, captain! We are putting the Indian on the rock!"

"Set her free!" came an answer. "Cut her bonds and let her go. At once, do you hear?" cried Peter, "or I'll plunge my hook in you!"

"Aye, aye!" said the pirates, quite puzzled. But they did as they were told, thinking it was Hook that was talking. Tiger Lily quickly slipped off the rock and swam away. No sooner had they freed the princess, when a voice came from behind, shouting: "Boat ahoy!" But it wasn't Peter's voice this time—it was the *real* Captain Hook who was speaking! He swam to the rock.

"Where is the Indian?" Hook demanded.

"We set her free, as you ordered," they said.

"I gave no such order!" Hook cried. "What dark spirit is afoot this night!"

Peter shouted out: "It is I, Peter Pan!" A fight then began between the lost boys and the pirates. The pirates were soon chased away and the boys made for shore with Wendy. Thinking Peter had

already left, they started for home. But Peter was still looking for Hook. And Hook was looking for Peter. They came face to face in the darkness on top of Marooner's Rock. There Hook injured poor Peter so bad he could not fly away. Just as he was

about to finish Peter off, Hook heard the *tick-tick-tick* of the crocodile, and quickly swam away in fright. Peter was left to drown, and would have done so, if the kind Neverbird had not swam out with her nest and rescued him.

In no time at all, Peter recovered from his injury. But greater danger still lay ahead. And it came on what would be known as the *Night of Nights*. Tinker Bell awoke from her fairy sleep to the sounds of a fierce and dreadful battle above.

The pirates were attacking the Indians, who had been guarding the secret cave to keep Peter safe till he got well. But in this battle, the Indians lost and were driven away. Then the evil Hook tricked the children hiding below by beating the

Indian's tom-tom, which the Indians always did when they had won a battle. One by one, the children were taken prisoner as they left the cave. Wendy was last, and Hook, with phony politeness, tipped his cap and bowed low to her. He did it in such a way that she was too fascinated to cry out. Afterall, she was only a little girl.

Hook ordered the children put on his ship.

All this time Peter was fast asleep, thinking the Indians had chased the pirates away. Hook slipped silently through the cave entrance and set his greedy gaze upon the bed where Peter lay in happy dreams. Seeing the bottle of medicine by Peter's bedside, he carefully uncorked it and poured a *deadly* poison inside. Then he wormed his way back out of the cave.

Peter slept on, unaware of the danger. Some time later, Tinker Bell flew in. Waking Peter, she told all that had happened.

"The Indians lost! Wendy and the boys taken prisoner! I'll rescue her! I'll rescue them all!" Then he thought of what he could do to please Wendy. He would take his medicine.

His hand closed on the fatal drink.

"No!" shrieked Tinker Bell. She had heard Hook laughing and talking of his evil deed with his men. No time for words now. A time for deeds! Quick as a flash, Tink flew between his lips and the deadly cup. She drank it all.

"What's the matter with you?" cried Peter.

"It was poison, Peter. And now I am going to be dead." She could barely move her wings now.

Peter flung out his arms to all the children who were dreaming at that time of the Neverland. "Do you believe in Neverland? Do you believe in fairies?" he cried. "If you believe, clap your hands; don't let Tinker Bell die!"

Many children clapped. Some didn't. And a few

little beasts hissed. The clapping children saved
Tink. You see, fairies can't live unless *someone*
believes in them. Tink never thought to thank the
children who believed, but she would have liked to
get at the ones who had hissed.

"And now to rescue Wendy!" said Peter. Darting through the moonlit trees, his knife at his side, he set out on his quest. Before long he found Hook's ship, the *Jolly Roger*. It was a spooky-looking boat, dirty and dark to the hull.

Hook had Wendy tied to the mast and was preparing to have the children walk the plank. He smiled at them with clenched teeth. He took a step toward Wendy. But he never reached her. For he clearly heard the sounds of *tick-tick-tick!*

It was the *terrible* sound of the crocodile.

The sound came closer and closer, as if the crocodile were boarding the ship! "Hide me! Hide me!" begged Hook. His crew gathered around him, while the boys ran to the side to see. It was no crocodile coming to help them. It was Peter. He was making the *tick-tick* sound in the hope he could board the ship. And it worked! He slipped over the side and then into the cabin, where he found weapons for the boys.

With sword drawn, he called to Hook, "Dark and evil man, let us fight!"

"Proud and bold child," said Hook, "prepare to meet thy doom!"

Without more words they began to fight.

Peter and Hook fought hard. At one time, Peter knocked Hook's sword from his hand. With a bow, Peter invited Hook to pick it up. He did so, but with a sad feeling that Peter was showing good manners. "It's some fiend fighting me!" cried Hook. "Pan, who and what art thou?"

"I'm youth! I'm joy!" Peter sang out. "I'm a little bird that has broken out of the egg!"

This, of course, was nonsense; but it was proof to the unhappy Hook that Peter did not know at all who or what he was. This Hook thought to be the best of good manners. Hook fought on, but now was without hope. He no longer asked for life, but desired only one thing in his dark heart: to see Peter use bad manners before it was cold forever.

Seeing Peter coming at him, Hook sprang to the side of the ship to throw himself into the sea.

He did not care that the crocodile was waiting for him. As he looked at Peter, he invited him with a wave to use his foot. This made Peter use his foot to kick at Hook rather than make a courtly stab with his sword. At last Hook got the upper hand

that he wanted so much.

"Bad manners," he cried jeeringly, and went content to the crocodile. Thus died Captain Hook. Peter Pan had finally beaten the pirates and brought peace to Neverland. For the day, at least.

There were *sure* to be other adventures just ahead. But for Wendy, John, and little Michael, it was time to go home. So, they set off at once and flew away from Neverland and back to the nursery where their mother was waiting.

"George! Nana!" Mrs. Darling called out when she saw the children. Mr. Darling and Nana came rushing into the room to share her joy. It was a lovely sight, but there was none to see it except a little boy and a tiny fairy who were staring in at the window. Peter Pan had many joys that other children can never know, but he was looking through the window at the one joy that he could never have—the *love* of a family.

The Darlings adopted the lost boys, and loved them as if they were their own. And Mrs. Darling promised Peter that Wendy could visit him every year.

Wendy waited for Peter's return. He didn't come for her until two years had passed. Although they had a grand time in the Neverland, the funny thing was that he didn't know that he had missed a year.

That was the last time the girl Wendy ever saw Peter. The years rolled on by without bringing Peter Pan. When they met again, Wendy was a married woman with a little girl of her own, named Jane.

One night, as Jane lay asleep, Wendy sat sewing in the nursery. The window blew open and Peter flew in. He hadn't changed at all. "Hello, Wendy," he said, not seeing any change.

"Oh, Peter!" she said with tears in her eyes, "I cannot fly with you anymore. I grew up long ago." Peter looked horrified. He sat on the floor and sobbed. Wendy left the room to try and think of what to do. Peter's sobbing woke little Jane, who sat up in her bed.

"Boy," Jane asked, "why are you crying?"

When Wendy returned to the nursery she found Peter sitting on the bedpost. He was crowing loudly as Jane flew around the room. In the end, of course, Wendy let them fly away together to

Neverland. And so it will continue with Jane's daughter, and her daughter, and her daughter, forevermore. It will last so long as children are happy, innocent, and heartless.